was 'referre

Dragon Vaults. Next door is Leesing's which can be seen in the photograph of the Market Place on page 6 and next door is the Albany Temperance Hotel.

Silver Street just after the turn of the century. Bower's Fold is on the right. The buildings on the left were demolished for road widening shortly afterwards.

Memory Lane Doncaster

3. High Street between 1909 — when the Danum Hotel was built — and 1912, when artificial tooth maker W Bolt had left number 57.

Researched and written by

John Tunney

and

Carol Hill

First published in 1989 by

Archive Publications Ltd
Carrington Business Park
Urmston
Manchester M31 4DD
in association with
The Doncaster Star
40 Duke Street
Doncaster DN1 3EA
and
Doncaster Library Service
Central Library
Waterdale, Doncaster DN1 3JE

Printed and bound in the United Kingdom by
Netherwood Dalton & Co. Ltd., Huddersfield

ISBN 0-948946-31-8

4. A Balby tram passes Cleveland Street before 1906. Up to then paperhanger Alfred Skinner was in business at number 192. The YMCA began life as the St James Hospital for the Plant workers in January, 1853.

Foreword

It is some years since the local newspaper (then the *Doncaster Evening Post*) produced a feature on Old Doncaster. With this in mind, and sensing the public's growing interest and awareness of its past, *The Star* decided that the time was right to produce an illustrative supplement reflecting Doncaster and its people in a bygone age.

Initially, it was anticipated that the Doncaster Central Library's illustrations collection would be but one of several sources to be searched for suitable material, but it soon became evident that photographs from that collection would form the basis for the entire supplement - to be called 'Memory Lane'. The Local History Librarian, Carol Hill worked closely with a *Star* special features team assisting and advising in the selection of photographs, and the research to captions.

The Memory Lane supplement, produced during the last three months of 1988, elicited a tremendous response from the public: further photographs were handed in, there were letters from delighted readers and much additional information was supplied about the photographs. In fact the joint project was such a resounding success that the decision was taken to publish the supplement in book form in association with Archive Publications of Manchester. It is hoped that this publication will both give pleasure to its readers and generate further information and source material for users of the Local History Library.

Everyone concerned in the publication of both the supplement and the book is to be congratulated.

John Chapman
Chief Librarian.

Introduction

It seems like an eternity since Doncaster was simply a place where the Deltic locomotive slowed down a bit but still went galloping through.

The train traveller would lift his head, admire what he thought was probably a cathedral and then get back to work as either London or Newcastle beckoned.

Little did he think that the town and its history over the last century or so would be something that could quite easily occupy every waking moment of the day and possibly some sleep time as well.

And even less that he would acquire a deepening affection for the place solely from digging into its past.

But, starting on 16 September last year, this is what has happened. I shoudn't be at all surprised. You never know what is coming next in journalism. What began in September 1988 as tentative steps in the production of a pictorial nostalgia trip has matured and grown.

Local history librarian Carol Hill knows the date well enough. It was her birthday. The present she got was assisting someone who knew next to nothing about the town in the production of first a newspaper supplement and then a book about it. Much of what has happened is thanks to her enthusiasm for the subject.

First, there was the growth of a relationship of trust between *The Star* and Doncaster Council in the form of its library service. This led to the tremendously popular *Doncaster Star* Memory Lane publication.

Second, there was the realisation that the people of the town themselves have a deep regard for their home. The interest in Memory Lane has been enormous. It has been a privilege to be involved in it.

Some of it has been hard work. There are a lot of hidden pitfalls in old photographs and checking exact dates can be very time-consuming and frustrating. It would be easy to take a year written on the back of a photograph as being accurate, but you don't necessarily know what led someone else to date it. Checking is advisable.

Sometimes you get lucky. In one of the photographs in this book we spotted a pub licensee's name. By sheer chance, he had only just taken over the licence, according to the trade directory. Thus we could prove that the date of the picture was 1903 and not 1902....assuming that the directory was right. In another, a rough date was established because of a newspaper poster mentioning the Russo-Japanese war.

When a precise date is established it can be quite exhilarating for the time detective. It all goes back to Mark Twain's dictum that work is something you have to do when you'd rather be doing something else. However, he also probably said something about pride coming before a fall. We've tried to be accurate in our captions, but if there are mistakes we apologize.

It is also certain that there are omissions. Sometimes it is impossible to date a picture or even to say exactly where it was taken.

We would love more information about the pictures in this book. We would also love to see more pictures of old Doncaster and its surrounding towns and villages.

We have tried to cover as wide a range of topics as possible. Some things we couldn't include. We have found very few interesting sporting pictures in the archives, for example. A subject like the railway and its influence on the town is very important and we have given it due weight. Which other town in England had a Plant that everyone knew simply as that?

In the course of this some faces have become very familiar. Army bandsman Fred Harrop springs to mind, as does the man in the rail mail sorting office and the baby in the pram in Silver Street. And the two policemen in St Sepulchre Gate - a street name that is indelibly stamped on my memory.

We owe thanks to the people and bodies who gave us permission to use photographs - Robert Walter and Gary Swann," Trustees of the Science Museum", London, and the National Railway Museum, York. And to David Banks and Phil Dalton of *Sheffield Newspapers* for their enthusiasm, advice and artistry.

John Tunney

6. *above:* The Market Place looking north about 1904. to the left is Scot lane and top left is Baxtergate. Killengrey's butterscotch shop is shown just before the business closed down. One of its neighbours was Leesing's, the pork butchers. In the 1920s the fish market replaced the stalls in the centre of the picture.

About Town

7. *left:* Baxtergate in the 1960s, pre-pedestrianisation. Only one foreign car is in sight and even then it's European. The buildings in the background were knocked down to make way for the Arndale Centre, later to become the Frenchgate Centre.

8. *above*: Inside Hodgson and Hepworth's store in St Sepulchre Gate about the turn of the century. The range of foodstuffs on display is now a rare sight. To be seen shopping there was a status symbol in the town.
9. below: The scene after the disastrous fire in January, 1901. When the shop opened its doors in 1872 it had a firm rule: no credit. At one stage 160 people were employed in many functions, baking and beer bottling among them. The business was taken over in the 1970s.

10. Three little maids from school are we. Striding out in the sunshine in St Sepulchre Gate between 1895 and 1903. We know it can't be later because Taylor's, the chemists on the left, became a hosiers in either 1902 or 1903. The tobacconists was Atkinson's and the butchers Dufty's.

11. In old views of Doncaster it's difficult to get away from sights of the parish church. This one shows St Sepulchre Gate before 1902. The monument to Patrick Stirling on the left is now on the approach to Hexthorpe Bridge.

12. St Sepulchre Gate with Aspinall's on the left and Scarborough's on the right, some time before 1902.

CUTLERY
TEA TABLE
AND
DESSERT
SPOONS

14. A wet night in the 1930s. The illuminated corner, then Harry Jacobs, was a favourite meeting place. The building was demolished and the site is now occupied by the Halifax Building Society.

15. *above* : Aspinall's tobacconists about the time of the Russo-Japanese war of 1904-5. Next door to the shop in St Sepulchre Gate were almshouses, the ancient St Thomas's hospital. The man pictured is Mr Aspinall. He worked for the Great Northern Railway, hence the uniform. His wife, photographed with him, ran the shop. In 1906 they moved to 23 West Street and the business closed about 1912. *13. left* : It wasn't until 1910 that policemen in the town were supplied with galoshes. This picture was taken at least eight years before that step. The two officers are in St Sepulchre Gate on a snowy day some time before 1902.

16. After St George's, the town's most familiar landmark: Clock Corner before 1894.

17. High Street before 1894. The corner of Priory Place may be under construction. Above first floor level the facades remain virtually unchanged. The handsome Brougham on the right is an 1880s design.

18. *below:* High Street as it used to be - the pace and bustle in this 1920s photograph can almost be felt.

19. The corner of Hallgate and Silver Street before 1912, when it was demolished and rebuilt as Prudential Chambers Corner. The St Leger Tavern is the tall building on the left in Silver Street. It was first referred to in 1841 and it's still there.

20.*below:* Silver Street, late twenties or early thirties. The new Palace theatre/cinema can be seen centre background.

21. Before the Clean Air Acts: this view north from St George's tower was taken at an unknown date. The Guildhall can be seen on the left.
22. *below:* In this shot the electricity power station can clearly be seen on the left. The system was switched on by the Mayoress on 2 April 1900.

23. Hamilton Lodge, where many citizens drew their first breath. It was a private house until the 1930s and was then taken over by a women's co-operative as a nursing home for working mums. It is now the area health authority's sports and social club.

Growing Up

24. Sunderland Street, Tickhill, with the wonderful pram virtually the only traffic.

25. Outside the Vine at Balby Bridge, small boys gather for the coach, or is it the camera ? The coach party - all men - appear to be setting off for the races. The photograph is thought to date from early this century.

26. Gentle instruction for a group of handicapped youngsters. The town's revolutionary Deaf and Dumb Institution opened in 1829, as one of the first special schools in the country. By 1905, when this picture was taken, its reputation had spread throughout Europe. It is now the Yorkshire Residential School for the Deaf and its present home opened in 1939.

27. Swimming at Water Lane, Tickhill. The 'pool' was normally a sheep dip, but that doesn't seem to bother the bathers!

28. Schoolboys' heroes. A triumphal return for Doncaster Rovers. The year is 1912, the date 16 March. The trophy they are bearing is the Sheffield Challenge Cup, won by defeating Sheffield United Reserves at Wath after a replay. Rovers got to the final by beating Barnsley Reserves, Wath and Rotherham County, scoring eleven goals and conceding only two in the process. Reed bagged two in the replay and Taylor scored the other in the 3-0 win. It was the second time they'd won the trophy. The first win was in 1891, oddly enough Sheffield United also being the losers.

29. Floods affected much of the region in May, 1932. This is the scene at Askern with kids enjoying the fun.

30. Waiting for the next instalment - a group of youngsters impatient for the opening of Wheatley library in the early fifties.

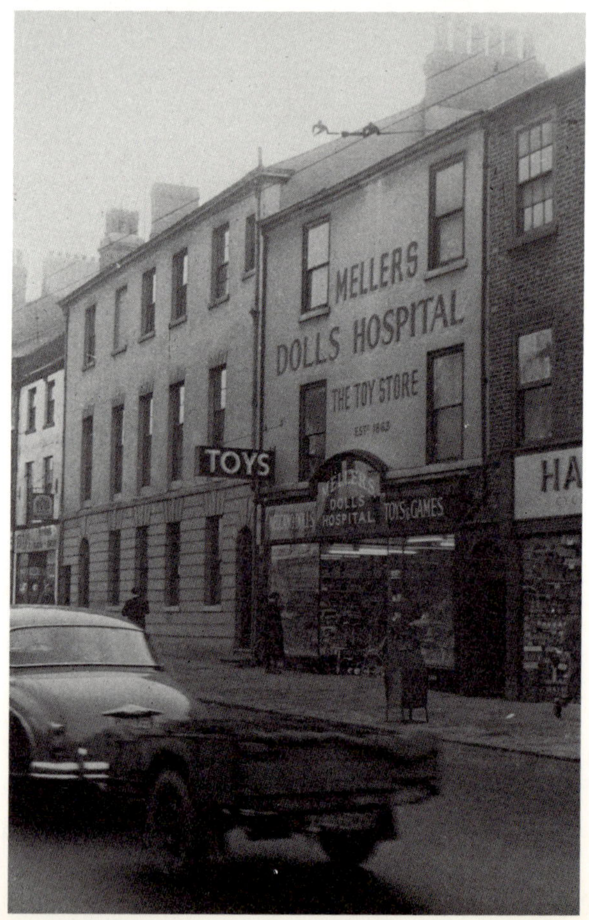

31. A shop with a special place in the memories of generations of girls. It opened in the 1920s and closed after half a century of mending dolls and one or two broken hearts.

Out and about

32. High Road, Balby, with the tollhouse that later became the library. The Wesleyan chapel in the background has long been demolished. The owner of the geese may have been the man in the straw hat. He ran Rose Farm, Warmsworth, and his name was Mr Fox.

33. *below:* Anchorage Farm, Sprotborough, 1894.

34. Shopfronts of yesteryear: the Hatfield branch of the Co-op in the mid twenties. Manager James Castle is flanked by two of his assistants.

35. *below:* The cycle shop at Askern, now a car showroom. Many people will better remember Claybourns in business at the corner of Waterdale and Hallgate from the early thirties to the sixties.

36. The Tickhill relief fund of 1895, set up by Miss Laughton and her sister Mrs Curtis to help people badly hit by an appalling spell of bad weather. On 23 January, 100 quarts of soup were distributed. On 10 February, a meeting was called by the vicar and the fund put on a more formal footing. The picture was probably taken at a house opposite the Red Lion.

37. Askern Spa at the turn of the century.

38. Tickhill Pond at an unknown date.

39. It wouldn't have been much fun for householders in Hunt Lane, Bentley, as the floods surged into their homes in the spring of 1932.

40. A policeman is on hand to ensure fair play at the water sports which used to be a feature of the June fair at Thorne. Walking the greasy pole was one of the challenges. This contestant didn't quite make it.

41. A tranquil scene of the kind beloved of Victorian and Edwardian photographers. Daisy chain making on Hexthorpe Flatts, date unknown.

42. The Great North Road looking north, date unknown.

Years of Work

43. *above:* Steam road engines travelled quite long distances for purposes such as harvesting and road making - in much the same way that earth-moving plant is hired for construction today. This machine was visiting the Doncaster area from its base at Bishopthorpe, York, on an unknown date.

44. *right:* Micklebring premises of shopkeeper John Boakes between 1908-1917.

45. *below:* The entrance to Hawksworth's Yard, off Duke Street, in the late nineteenth century. James Butterfield was living at number Nine in 1891. There were chimney sweeps by the name of Butterfield operating from St Sepulchre Gate as far back as 1837.

46. *above* : Askern Main pit before the Great War.

47. We don't know who the man with the spade was, but it's unlikely he did much digging with it. The dignitaries are at the ceremonial start of Hatfield pit.

48. The cutting of the first sod at Hatfield Main pit on 11 October 1911. It's hard to believe that it was done by hand. It took five years for the shaft to reach the Barnsley bed at 852 yards below ground level.

49. It looks like pay time at Brodsworth Colliery, probably Great War era. The first sod was cut in 1905, but production did not begin for several years.

50. Victorian blacksmiths take a break from work to pose for the camera at Hatfield.

51. The Plant workers of the Great Northern Railway were drafted in for service in both world wars. In 1916 women worked shifts and Sundays to produce cases for six inch, 100lb artillery shells.

52. Women stepped in to do jobs normally filled by men. Carriage cleaning was one of them.

53. Instead of shells, glider wings formed the World War Two effort for these women.

54. *overleaf:* In 1939-45 women took up painting of rolling stock.

SMOKING
SMOKING
L C
3
3

The days of steam

55. An unidentified locomotive in the area, possibly 1855.

56. The locomotive *Marshall* remains a mystery, but the buildings in the background are clearly Doncaster station.

57. A Stirling 2-4-0 at Hexthorpe Bridge. Patrick Stirling was chief engineer of the Great Northern Railway and more than 700 locomotives were built at the Plant to his designs. This one was built in 1886 and withdrawn from service in 1923.

58. *above:* A common sight at the height of popularity of the St Leger. Dozens of excursion trains are lined up, steam at the ready, waiting to take racegoers back home.

59. *left:* A large-boilered Ivatt Atlantic at the south end of Doncaster station about 1910.

60. A *Pom Pom,* one of 174 Great Central 9Js built. They first took to the rails in 1901 and the class swiftly acquired their nickname because the sound of their exhausts was thought to resemble the rapid-fire gun. This one is probably at Mexborough in 1910.

61. One of the railway sorting vans built at the plant for the Post Office. This one, pictured about 1900, is thought to have been constructed in 1885.

62. A gathering of London & North Eastern Railway bigwigs at the Eden Grove sports ground in the late 1920s. Sir Nigel Gresley, chief designer, is pictured front left . Next to him is chairman Sir William Whitelaw. On the right is Sir Ralph Wedgwood and second left, back row, is Arthur Peppercorn.

63. The naming of the *Great Northern* marke the end of the railway, not the beginning. Th amalgamations of 1922 made it part of th LNER. Many railway fans think this and it partner *Sir Frederick Banbury* the mos beautiful locomotives built at Doncaster.

64. Sir Nigel Gresley's 'hush hush' loco, th prototype of the streamlined Pacifics, built i 1929.

65. The 2000th locomotive built at the Plant. It was unveiled in 1943.

66. *Doncaster Rovers* at home getting a wash and brush up. The class B17s with the names of football clubs often had their nameplates changed for publicity reasons. The *Sunderland*, for example, which hauled the 1937 FA cupwinners back to Wearside was actually *Derby County* with the out-of-action *Sunderland's* plate displayed.

7. This was the last steam locomotive built in the town. The date is 14 October 1957, and with the engine are the men who built it. Most of the sign work for this type (Standard Class 4, 2-6-0) was done in Doncaster.

Horse Power

68. Hodgson and Hepworth's horse-drawn bus. In 1889 it ran every half hour to Balby and Bentley and hourly to Hexthorpe, Bennetthorpe, Christ Church, Regent Square and Race Common. The fare was 1d or half a new penny.

69. The Balby Road laundry opened by Sarah Gardom in 1897. JW Whaley became a partner in 1901 and he is possibly the man on the left. The Doncaster and District Laundry was next door.

70. One of the few pictures of the Bagshaw photographic studio. We are indebted to Luke Bagshaw for the many pictures he took of everyday life. His father John, already in business as a grocer, opened it in 1897.

71. Station Road in the snow between 1899 and 1902. There are no trams, but the Grand Theatre is still there and the corner that became known as Priestnall's.

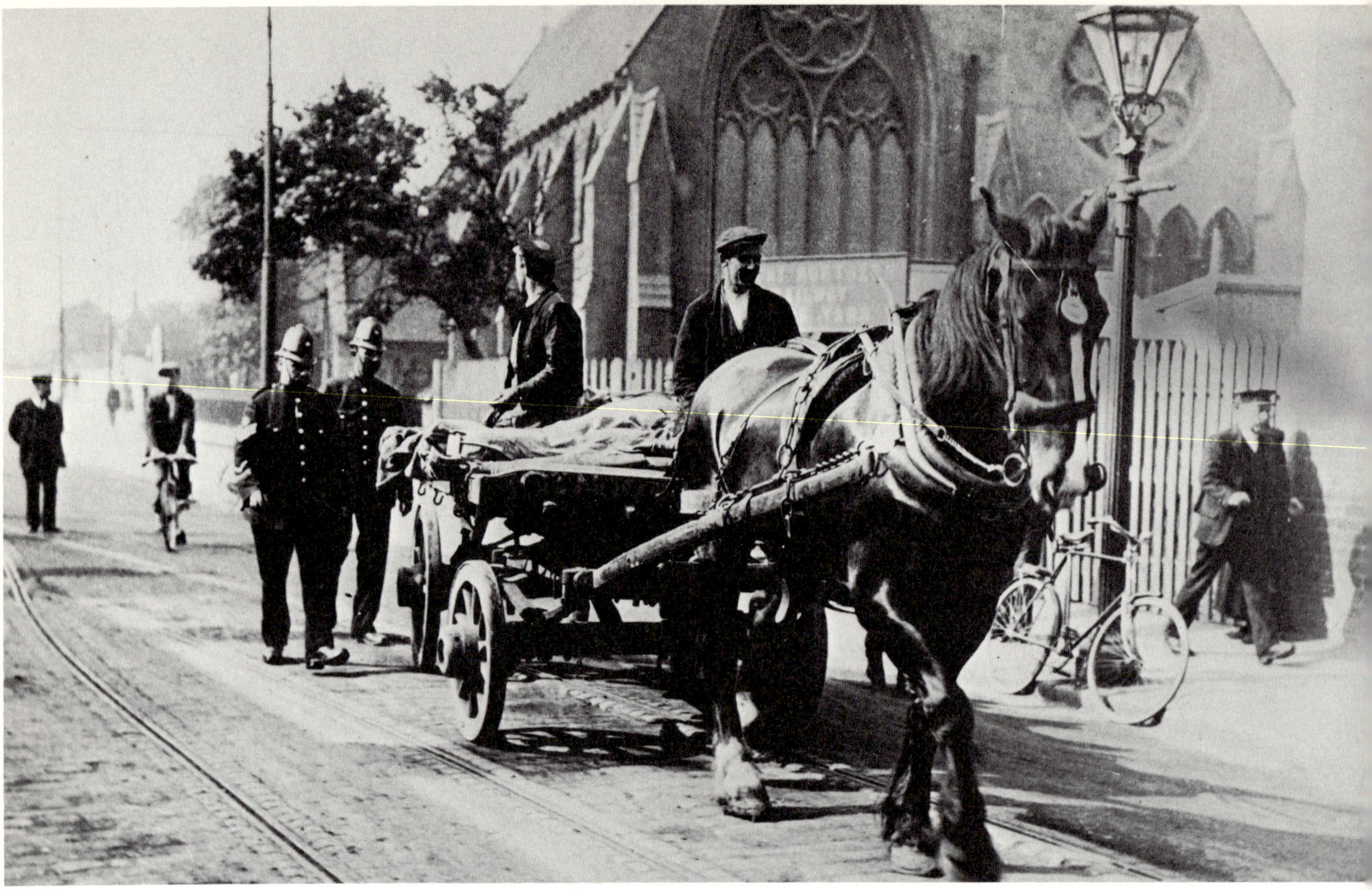

72. A scene that must have been very familiar around the area. A Great Northern wagon with police 'escort' heads towards town with St James's Church — the 'Plant Church' — in the background. It was built by Sir Edmund Denison, the railway's chairman, and consecrated in 1858.

73. Frank Pickering's brewery was one of many small outfits in the area. The first reference to it is in 1907 and the last in 1917. It was based in Back Lane, Balby, now Sandford Road.

Vintage Transport

74. South Parade. In the early days there was a tram to the race course every ten minutes.

75. St Leger week in 1903. The Ram Hotel on the right was demolished in 1909 and the Danum built in its place.

76. A tram, possibly at Warmsworth or Bentley, decorated for the coronation of George V in 1911.

77. A Panhard car making the last trip over the Marshgate level crossing on 7 February 1910. Driver was GE Smith and passengers Mayor J Halmshaw, Alderman JF Clark, Councillor George Smith and Miss Smith.

78. North Bridge in 1910, the year it was built. Before construction, the Marshgate level crossing caused considerable congestion. The Bentley tram previously had to terminate there.

The tram sheds at Greyfriars Road. The plaque on the wall now at the National Tramways Museum at Crich, Derbyshire. Wyld, transport manager from 1902-1904, is believed to be man standing next to the driver.

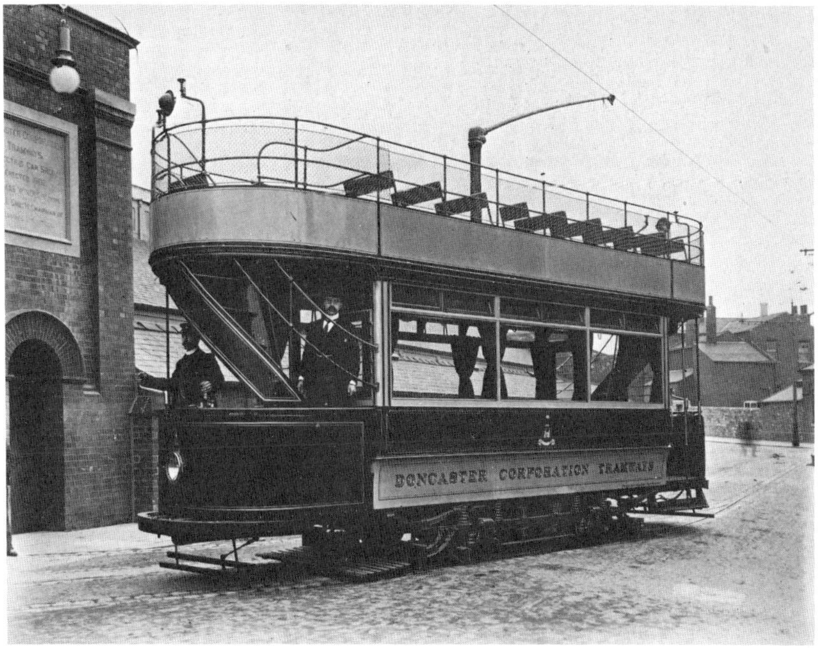

80. The Brodsworth tram coming up Frenchgate from the depot, probably late 1920s. On the right is the garage where the Cheswold car was designed and built. In 1914 a four cylinder machine of 15.9 horsepower cost £450.

1. Warmsworth-bound tram outside Jubilee Buildings in St Sepulchre Gate, 1920s.

82. *above*: Pell's Close, off Printing Office Street in the 1920s. The dashing motor cyclist has not been identified.

83. *right:* Steadman's Taxis in Princes Street. First reference to the cab firm can be found in 1877.

84. *below:* Smith's Royal Carriageworks. The company was established in 1805, but elsewhere. First Doncaster reference is 1877, in St Sepulchre Gate. It moved to West Laith Gate in 1891. The car may be a Mass, built in France between 1903 and 1923.

85. Jackson's garage, birthplace of the Cheswold car. WY 4293 is a two-seater green Wolseley, however. It was registered by EA Jackson in 1922, transferred to AH Wilson in 1930 and scrapped the following year.

War and Peace

86. A mystery picture. A squadron of cavalry photographed in High Street. It purports to show Boer War soldiers, but the date of 1896 it bears does not tally with the South African conflict of 1899-1902. Also the clock at Clock Corner in the background was replaced by the present clock in 1894.

87. The return of troops from South Africa after the Boer War. They belong to the 2nd Battalion, York and Lancaster Regiment, and the Hallamshire Rifles. Many were local men from Doncaster, others were from Rotherham, Barnsley and Pontefract.

. Another mystery. The photograph bears the ords 'Military Sunday', but we have no nowledge of what this means, although the ldiers are locally based dragoons.

89. More Military Sunday, with the same dragoons. Fred Harrop, from Sheffield, second left in front row, is playing the trombone. The picture was taken by the Regina company, which operated between 1908 and 1923.

). Fred Harrop, *extreme left*, is pictured with ome of his band colleagues. He was a regular orrespondent with his family in Ellesmere Road, heffield.

91. York and Lancaster Regiment veteran
return from the Boer War.

92. Doncaster Territorial parade at
Sprotbrough church, 15 November 1908.

93. More Territorials, this time in Sunday b
at Bentley.

94. The Home Guard at the Plant works in December, 1944. The rolling stock in the background is ancient Great Central.

95. The fire brigade at the Plant, date unknown.

96. The Conisbrough Fire Brigade proudly hold a shield won in a hydrant drill competition against other local teams. According to Cecil Ogilwy, himself a member of the Conisbrough brigade in the twenties and thirties, the date was 1901 and the picture was taken in Church Street. Front left is Captain Jones, a blacksmith. Top right is Tom Senior and the others he names as Downing, Rogers, Walker, Gregory, Uttley, Hotson and Gabbitas.

97. The roller skating rink opened on 16 August 1909, at 7 pm. It cost 6d (two and a half pence) admission to one of the best rinks in the country. The earlier arena burned down on Boxing Day, 1876.

98. Doncaster Rovers some time shortly after they moved to Belle Vue in 1922. The man in the cap on the left is probably trainer W Russell. Second from right could be director A Thomson, while players identified include goalkeeper Jacklin.

99. St George's old church burned down on 28 February 1853, and was replaced five years later. This engraving takes a little artistic licence; the pinnacles on the tower don't exactly match reality.

front cover: Almost certainly the opening day of the tram system on Monday, 2 June 1902. A procession of three cars took to the rails at about 12.30pm. This picture was taken in Station Road not long before the ceremonial lunch at the Mansion House (men only). Guests dined on mock turtle soup, salmon, lobster, chicken, ham, lamb, beef and duck, with corporation tart for pudding. Townspeople fought to get on the trams, which did not stop running until 2.15 the next morning. Nearly a quarter of the population of 39,000 travelled. Receipts? £43.